W9-AYJ-840

For Dylan, with all my love x
~T C

For Karyn Anderton
~T M

This edition published by Scholastic Inc.,
557 Broadway, New York, NY 10012,
by arrangement with Little Tiger Press.
Scholastic and associated logos
are trademarks and/or registered
trademarks of Scholastic Inc.
Scholastic Canada Ltd.; Markham, Ontario

Original edition published in English by Little Tiger Press,
an imprint of Magi Publications, London, England, 2011

Text copyright © Tracey Corderoy 2011
Illustrations copyright © Tina Macnaughton 2011

All rights reserved. No part of this book may be reproduced
in any manner, except for brief quotations in critical articles
or reviews, without permission.

ISBN: 978-1-84895-221-8

Printed in China • LTP/1800/0138/1010

2 4 6 8 10 9 7 5 3 1

Little Duckling Lost

Tracey Corderoy • Tina Macnaughton

HASTINGS PUBLIC LIBRARY
227 EAST STATE ST
HASTINGS MI 49058

One breezy day, four little ducklings were making a daisy chain.

"Pick and thread!" chanted Polly, Molly, and Holly.

"Look at me!" chuckled Dylan, all tied up in a big flowery knot!

"Now," said Mommy, "we're off to the pond for your very first swim. Hold on to the daisy chain so you won't get lost."

"It's a choo-choo chain!" cried Dylan. "Choo-choo!"

Polly, Molly, Holly, and Dylan skipped along behind
Mommy, singing a springtime song . . .

"*Four little ducklings all in a row,*
Skipping across the bridge we go!
Wiggle our tails—we're on our way
Down to the pond to splash and play!"

Suddenly, the ducklings spotted a beautiful, blue feather.

"So pretty!" gasped Polly, Molly, and Holly.

"Come back!" cried Dylan as the feather blew away.

Then he had a *wonderful* idea . . .

On the other side of the bridge, some baby lambs were playing catch-the-petals.

"*We* want to play, too!" said Polly.

"All right," smiled Mommy. She counted her ducklings as they hopped off the bridge. "Polly, Molly, Holly, and . . .

"OH, MY!" she gasped.
"Where's Dylan?"

All in a fluster
and a flap, everyone
searched for Dylan.

Suddenly, Molly spotted him stuck up a tree!
"Surprise!" cried Dylan. "I got the pretty
feather for you!"

"Oh, *Dylan*," said Mommy. "You *are* a sweetie!
But what did Mommy say about not getting lost?
Now, hold on to the choo-choo chain."
"And don't let go!" quacked Polly.

On they went into the woods, singing their song . . .

"Four little ducklings all in a row,
Counting the flowers as we go!
Flutter our wings—we're on our way
Down to the pond to dive and play!"

"Mmmm, *lovely!*" cried the girls, sniffing the flowers.
"A-ccchhhoooo!" sneezed Dylan.
Then he had a *wonderful* idea . . .

At the top of a hill, some baby hedgehogs
were playing roly-poly!

"*We* want to roll, too!" said Polly.

"All right," smiled Mommy. She counted
her ducklings as they tumbled down the hill.
"Polly, Molly, Holly, and . . .

"WAIT!" she flapped. "Where's Dylan?"

With wings a-flutter and
feathers flying, everyone
searched for Dylan.
Then suddenly a whirlwind of
fluff came spinning toward them . . .

"Surprise!" cried Dylan. "I picked some pretty flowers for you!"

"Oh, *Dylan,*" said Mommy. "You *are* kind! But you forgot what Mommy told you *again* . . ."

"Don't let go of the daisy chain!" yelled his sisters.

On they waddled under a hedge, and *at last* they saw . . .

. . . the pond!

"*Phew!*" gasped Mommy.

"All safely here!"

Polly, Molly, and Holly dipped their
toes into the water.

"But it's *c-c-cold*!" they shivered.

"We don't like it!"

Then suddenly,

splash!

Dylan was in . . .

. . . and – *wow* – this was *fun*!

"Look!" cried Dylan. "Look at me!"
He splished and splashed and swam
and swam until, all too soon, it was
time to go.

On the way home, Dylan felt so very clever! He could *swim* and Mommy had said he was great! He yawned, as a big, silver moon lit the sky, and he and his sisters sang one final song . . .

"*Four sleepy ducklings all in a row,*
Waddling back for tea we go.
Tiny stars begin to peep,
Soon we'll all be fast asleep . . ."

When they got home, Mommy toasted muffins for tea. Then she counted her ducklings at the table.

"Polly, Molly, Holly, and . . . Oh, *dear*," she sighed. "Not again! *Where's Dylan?*"

Polly wriggled, Molly giggled, and Holly
whispered in Mommy's ear. Then they
peeped around the door . . .

. . . and there, curled up in his
choo-choo chain, was *Dylan*.
"Night-night," giggled his
sisters as he gave a tiny snore.
"Sleep tight," whispered Mommy.
"Sweet dreams!"